THE OLD MAN
AT THE MOAT

All inquiries should be addressed to:
Barron's Educational Series, Inc.
250 Wireless Boulevard
Hauppauge, NY 11788

International Standard Book Number 0-8120-1097-3

Library of Congress Catalog Card Number 94-36090

Library of Congress Cataloging-in-Publication Data

Foster, Kelli C.
   The old man at the moat / by Kelli C. Foster and Gina Clegg
   Erickson : illustration by Kerri Gifford.
      p. cm—(Get ready—get set—read!)
   Summary: An old man in a yellow coat must tote a goat, a coyote,
   and a bag of oats across the moat in his boat.
   ISBN 0-8120-1097-3
      (1. Staries in rhyme.) I. Erickson, Gina Clegg. II. Gifford,
   Kerri, ill. III. Title. IV. Series: Erickson, Gina Clegg. Get
   ready—get set—read!
   P27, F8155Val   1994
   (E)—dc20   94-36090
                                                                   CIP
                                                                    AC

PRINTED IN HONG KONG
5678   9927   987654321

GET READY...GET SET...READ!

THE OLD MAN
AT THE MOAT

by
Foster & Erickson

Illustrations by
Kerri Gifford

BARRON'S

There once was an old man
in a yellow coat...

who had a little goat,
a coyote, and a bag of oats.

He had to tote the little goat, the coyote,

and the bag of oats
across the moat in his boat.

Only two could fit in
the boat.

With more in the boat,
it would not float.

How could he take them all
across the moat...

so the coyote would not
eat the goat, and the goat
would not eat the oats?

The old man in the
yellow coat wrote notes
in the sand.

Soon he had a plan
on how to take them
across the moat.

First, he took the goat over
the moat and went back.

Then he took the oats
over the moat
and brought the goat back.

Then he took the coyote
over the moat...

and went back to get
the goat.

Now he could gloat.
He got all three
across the moat!

The End

The OAT Word Family

boat
coat
float
gloat
goat
moat
oats

The OTE Word Family

coyote
notes
tote
wrote

Sight Words

who
only
over
soon
could
there
would
across
little
yellow
brought

Dear Parents and Educators:

Welcome to *Get Ready...Get Set...Read!*

We've created these books to introduce children to the magic of reading.

Each story in the series is built around one or two word families. For example, *A Mop for Pop* uses the OP word family. Letters and letter blends are added to OP to form words such as TOP, LOP, and STOP. As you can see, once children are able to read OP, it is a simple task for them to read the entire word family. In addition to word families, we have used a limited number of "sight words." These are words found to occur with high frequency in the books your child will soon be reading. Being able to identify sight words greatly increases reading skill.

You might find the steps outlined on the facing page useful in guiding your work with your beginning reader.

We had great fun creating these books, and great pleasure sharing them with our children. We hope *Get Ready...Get Set...Read!* helps make this first step in reading fun for you and your new reader.

Kelli C. Foster, PhD
Educational Psychologist

Gina Clegg Erickson, MA
Reading Specialist

Guidelines for Using *Get Ready...Get Set...Read!*

Step 1.   Read the story to your child.

Step 2.   Have your child read the Word Family list aloud several times.

Step 3.   Invent new words for the list. Print each new combination for your child to read. Remember, nonsense words can be used (*dat, kat, gat*).

Step 4.   Read the story *with* your child. He or she reads all of the Word Family words; you read the rest.

Step 5.   Have your child read the Sight Word list aloud several times.

Step 6.   Read the story *with* your child again. This time he or she reads the words from both lists; you read the rest.

Step 7.   Your child reads the entire book to you!

There are five sets of books in the

Series. Each set consists of five **FIRST BOOKS**
and two **BRING-IT-ALL-TOGETHER BOOKS**.

SET 1

is the first set your children should read.
The word families are selected from the short vowel sounds:
at, **ed**, **ish** and **im**, **op**, **ug**.

SET 2

provides more practice
with short vowel sounds:
an and **and**, **et**, **ip**, **og**, **ub**.

SET 3

focuses on
long vowel sounds:
ake, **eep**, **ide** and **ine**, **oke** and **ose**, **ue** and **ute**.

SET 4

introduces the idea that the word family sounds
can be spelled two different ways:
ale/ail, **een/ean**, **ight/ite**, **ote/oat**, **oon/une**.

SET 5

acquaints children with word families that
do not follow the rules for long and short vowel sounds:
all, **ound**, **y**, **ow**, **ew**.